15 ways
to go to bed
ways

Kathy Henderson

FRANCES LINCOLN

For Charley and Daniel

First published in paperback in Great Britain in 1989 by
Frances Lincoln Limited, 4 Torriano Mews,
Torriano Avenue, London NW5 2RZ

First hardback edition published in Great Britain in 1986 by
Macdonald and Co. (Publishers) Ltd.

British Library Cataloguing in Publication Data
available on request

ISBN 0-7112-0589-2

Printed in Hong Kong

9 8 7 6 5 4 3 2

Every which way

'Do you know 10 ways to go to bed?'

'I can tell you 15 standing on my head.

There's crawling, hopping, walking on your hands,
backflips, cartwheels, one over the other leapfrog
and when all those floor ways start to get boring
you can fling a flying jump from the chest of drawers.

There's fast asleep, wide awake, in a furious temper
or yawning warm from a long hot bath.
There's slithering shivering in between the clean sheets
fighting, crying, trying not to laugh and . . . . .'

'That's 15 ways to go to bed.'

'. . . but I haven't even started yet!'

Making beds

Jim Jones was in the habit
of making beds
all day and everywhere
in the broom cupboard
under the stairs.
(He put his toys
in cardboard box beds.)
Not that he was tired, but nests
were what Jim Jones liked making best.

He made one on the outhouse roof
another in the apple tree
and lay there watching for the stars
beyond the street lights.

He slung a hammock in the hall
and pitched a tent in the back yard
so he could listen to the rain
snapping on the canvas.

And then he left it for an hour or two
to climb the tree and slide downstairs.
When he came back he found the cat
had had her kittens there.

Jim Jones made beds.
Rather than cars or electric trains,
cooking, dolls or submarines
Jim Jones played beds.

Making places
   with a pillow and a blanket,
finding spaces
   in a corner, on a dustbin,
anywhere
to lie undisturbed
and dream.

Goodnight

Bedtime starts when the flannel flies
out of the bath on to the floor
for the third time. SPLAT!
'That's it! Everybody out!'

So it's us out
ducks out
rub down
pyjamas on
brush teeth, brush hair
mop the floor and up the stairs.

'Can we have a story?'
'I want this one!'
'Go on.
Sing us a song.'

It's hugs for us and hugs for her
then the click of the light by the bedroom door.

And it's
'Goodnight. Sleep tight.
Snuggle undercover till the morning light.
Yes, I said its bedtime. That's right.
Goodnight. Sleep tight.'

Excuses

But then it's
excuses, excuses, a million and more excuses
in that goodnight stretching, parent-catching bedtime song.

There's
'Don't shut the door Dad. It's dark in here.'

'Mum! Mum! I can't find my bear!
I thought you said it was under my bed'

and
'I'm thirsty, I'm thirsty.
Please can I have a drink of water?'
starting quiet and getting louder
'Please can I have a
drink of-can-I-have-a-drink-of
CAN I HAVE A DRINK OF WAAAATER!'

Then there's 'I feel sick,'

and 'I thought you called me!'

'I forgot to feed the goldfish,'

and 'I just need a wee,
it must have been that drink I think'

and — this is a good one —
'I heard a noise Mum
In our room
a knocking in the house noise
it could have been a mouse noise
but it could have been a burglar.
Mum will you come?'

And there's always one more.
You've just thought of it I'm sure.

Getting busy

Charley Barley's gone to bed.
He said goodnight
switched out the light
lay down flat
but
after a dozing, dazing while
he suddenly remembered
important things unfinished.
So it's out of bed
light on
behind the door
building on the floor
paper and scissors
staples and glue
no time for sleep
there's too much to do.

Midnight
and the light's still on.
There are paperclips, staples,
bricks and board
rearing, staggering into the air
but Charley Barley's asleep on the floor.

Sam Smith

When Sam Smith goes to bed
he puts his feet up on his pillow
and parks his head down under the covers
at the foot end.
Yes, he says, it's hot and dark.
Yes, he says, it can get smelly
but he'd rather lie there on his belly
buried in his rabbit burrow
than have the air mess with his hair
and besides, he says,
feet need to breathe.

Forgotten

If you don't want to go to bed
play dead, says Jo.
Lie low behind the sofa
keep quiet and out of sight
and, if you're lucky, they'll forget.

When everyone's busy
and you stay in the shadows
you can do what you want, says Jo.

You can hunt monsters under the carpet,
have a wrestling match with a dinosaur,
sing songs (softly)
to rock your dolls to sleep
or keep a fleet of space-ships waiting
by the floorboard shore.

Oi! Hang on a minute!
They're turning out the lights.
They're going upstairs.
What about me?
Anyone would think I wasn't here!

Bed clothes

Cousin Mary came to stay
and when I saw her next day
it was early
she was wearing
a long pink frilly nylon thing
fastened with ribbons round her neck.
It flapped around her in a panic
like some mad goldfish dressed in feathers.
She had pink puff-balls on her feet too.
'How do you do,' said cousin Mary.
I was trying not to stare
How on earth did she sleep in that lot?
Is that what other people wear?

Grandpa has big striped pyjamas
tied with string around his middle.
Dad and mum wear nothing at all
and as for us, well
we've had pyjamas, we've had nighties,
we've had zip-up suits with feet,
some were smooth and some were furry
but none were the least
like cousin Mary's
frilly bedtime nightdress thing.

Monsters

Underneath the blankets
down by your feet,
you know those crumbs that wriggle
and wrinkles that start to creep
as you're falling asleep . . . .
Are you sure that's the sheet
by your left big toe?
Isn't that prickly patch in the corner
beginning to grow?

You've got your arms here
your legs there,
your body and your head
and there's something come to get you
from the bottom of the bed.
Watch out!

Your hands have gone heavy.
There's humming in your ears.
Don't blink, don't breathe,
pretend you're not there
and just as you're turning purple
and you think you're going to burst
great claws grab your ankles,
you gasp
then you're screaming
kicking, thrashing,
are you dreaming?
What . . . ?   After all that
                                it's only the cat.

Winter and summer

I can't sleep. I won't sleep. I can't sleep
unless . . .
unless I can be in your bed with you
unless I have a story, another story and a song
unless I have both socks on
unless I have 4 bears, 3 dolls and my porcupine
   in bed with me
and I can see, so please leave the light on.
It's so dark outside. Winter and the rain
are beating on the window panes.

I won't sleep. I can't sleep. I won't sleep
because . . .
because it's summer
because it's light outside (this blind doesn't fool me)
because I can hear cars and buses
   and a blackbird singing from a rooftop TV aerial
because I'm lonely
because I'm hot
because mum's not home yet.

You're still up anyway. So why
should I
go to sleep?

Sick bed

Sarah Snudgit started sneezing
then she went all hot and cold
knees like jelly, shivers creeping
up her back and taking hold
like a bandage tightly squeezing
round her throat and through her head.
Sarah Snudgit wasn't feeling well
and so she went to bed.

She had
a cold drink
a warm blanket
an extra pillow under her head
a thermometer in a glass
a bottle of pink medicine
a bowl of fruit
and a book to read.

But it didn't feel like night
and it wasn't really day.
She couldn't get comfortable however she lay.
She wasn't awake and she wasn't asleep
and she didn't want anything much to eat.
Sarah Snudgit just lay low
and waited for the bug to go.

My friend Nita

My friend Nita came to stay last night.
She brought a suitcase with her nightdress
and her talking doll and a toothbrush. She lives next door.
We made her bed next to my bed on some cushions on the floor.
She says that our house smells different from hers.

My friend Nita came to stay last night.
We went to bed early but we stayed awake late talking.
She said that her bed wasn't a bed but a spaceship
    like that one on TV
and mine was another only it had a hole in it
so she was going to rescue me. And she did.
She climbed along the bookshelf!

My friend Nita came to stay last night.
We had a feast under the blankets
an apple each and some old sweets
left over from my birthday. They tasted a bit funny.
She said she had a tummy ache and she wanted her mum
but then she had a better idea.

So when my friend Nita came to stay last night
we had a romp and then a pillow fight. She started it
but when I threw mine at her it burst a bit
and there were feathers everywhere
they looked like snow in her hair and we couldn't
stop laughing.

We decided we weren't going to go to sleep at all
Then suddenly it was this morning.

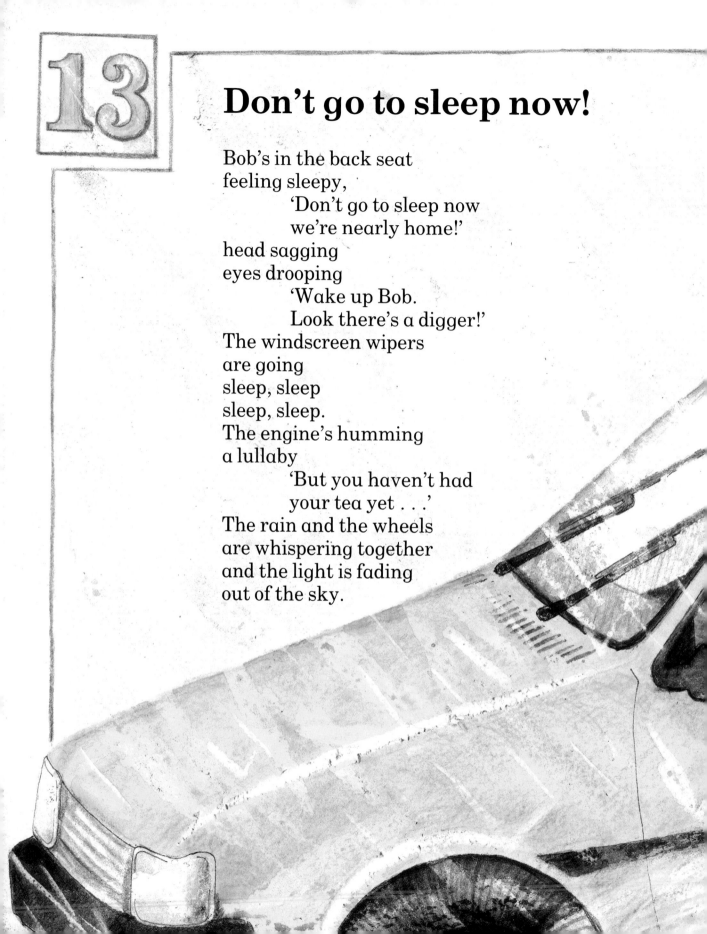

13

Don't go to sleep now!

Bob's in the back seat
feeling sleepy,
    'Don't go to sleep now
    we're nearly home!'
head sagging
eyes drooping
    'Wake up Bob.
    Look there's a digger!'
The windscreen wipers
are going
sleep, sleep
sleep, sleep.
The engine's humming
a lullaby
    'But you haven't had
    your tea yet . . .'
The rain and the wheels
are whispering together
and the light is fading
out of the sky.

The babysitter

We knew we wouldn't like her.
We didn't want dad to go.
And there was all that stuff about bed by eight
and teeth and hair and don't forget the baby's feed
and you've got to read your reading book for school tomorrow.

Dan painted his face purple stripes
Sal ran off and hid
The baby cried and I decided I'd had quite enough
of babysitters.

But none of it seemed to bother her
She didn't even yell
She just sat down in the big armchair
and started to tell a story by the fire.

After that I can't remember much
except the things she said
and the flicker of the firelight
and everything going very quiet.

She didn't make us listen,
she didn't have a book,
she just pulled strange stories from the air
and wrapped them round us, sprawling there

and I can't remember arguing,
I can't remember bed,
just waking trails of drifting dreams
twisting in my head.

The night before

It's the night before, the night before
can't wait to go to bed because
tomorrow is THE DAY.
They rush to undress
and into bed in record time
because tomorrow is tomorrow,
is only a night away.

But have you ever tried
to go to sleep in a hurry?

The minutes are crawling,
each one is sprawling, more and more slowly.
Lloyd is shifting, twisting on the top bunk,
wide awake dreaming of to-mor and to-mor
and tomorrow
while next door there's music playing
and in the road the traffic roars.

'Shut up. I can't sleep.
Your sheet's hanging down in my face.'
Underneath, John can't wait.
Tomorrow feels like grit in the bedclothes,
crumbs in the sheets
and across the room there's *pop pop,*
Stevie is sucking his thumb,
Pop each time he takes a breath
Pop will tomorrow ever come?

'Lloyd?'
'Yes?'
'Sssh.'
'What if?'
'Sssh! I'm trying to go to sleep.'

Three together
getting later and later
waiting for the big day
trying to will the night away.